The Three Rulers and Echo

Author
Fuad A. Kamal

Illustrator
Piotr Antoniak

Once upon a time, there was a little robot named Robot. Robot awoke in a very dark forest. Robot was so lonely that even when the night came out, it had no stars. Robot felt so lost.

"Wait! Wait! Wait! This is a TERRIBLE story! Who is writing this?" asks Robot.

"Guilty as charged," replies Dr. Ducktopotamus, "But this is so unusual and exciting. My characters never talk to me!"

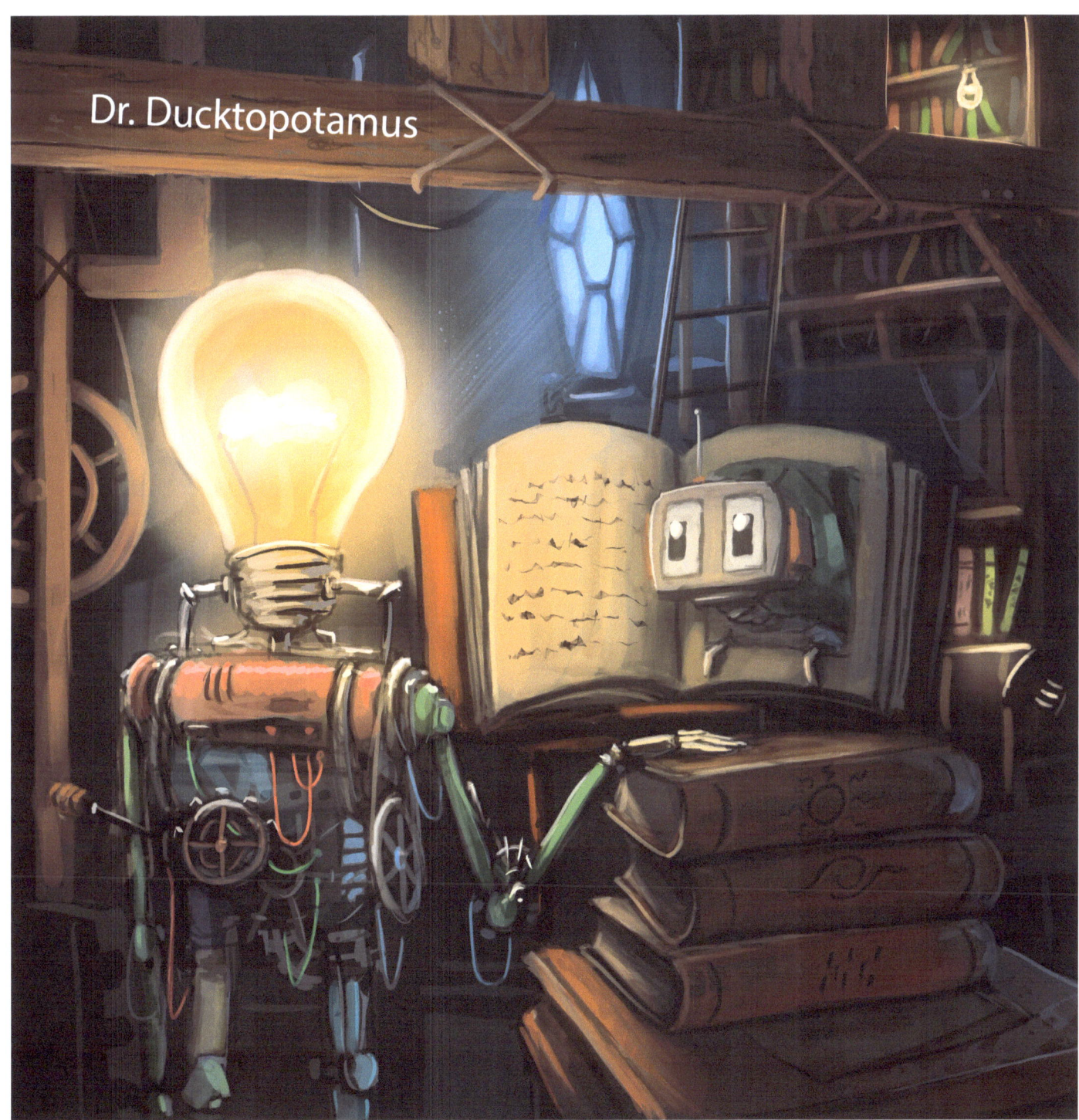

Robot sees three books in Dr. Ducktopotamus's collection: a sun book, a wind book, and a rain book.

"Why would anyone care for the wind or rain? I'll take the sun any day!" exclaims Robot.

"Well, things are not always what they seem," says Dr. Ducktopotamus. "Okay, Robot, back to the story..."

So Robot pulls in a sun called Compassion.

"This is much better. Hi. Do you have a name?" asks Robot.

"Hi. Call me Compassion," replies the sun.

Robot explores the land...

"Who are you?" asks Robot.

"We are this land's farmers, but we cannot seem to produce many crops," replies the tractor.

"My friend, the sun, will help you. Compassion will shine more brightly and bring forth the harvest for this land," says Robot.

However to his horror, Robot finds that, in this ineffective world, the more Compassion burns brightly, the more the farm tools leave their work and take to their chairs to rest and soak in the sun.

"How will you get any food if you just relax in the sun?" asks Robot.

"But it is such a nice day, even the king must rest," replies the spade, who was the king of the tools.

Robot kicks out the sun, exclaiming, "Anybody else would be better!"

Then Robot pulls in a rain cloud called Truth.

"What's your name?" asks Robot.

"Hi. Call me Truth," the rain cloud responds.

It rains and rains and rains. Out of the ensuing flood giant vines emerge with huge thorns sticking out. Robot is dejected and wonders about a world with only Truth in it. Will it be a sharp and insensitive world?

"Okay maybe I should not have kicked the sun out. Please send the sun back," sighs Robot.

Thus, Compassion joins Truth, as Robot looks on.

"Don't worry. I'll dry things up," says Compassion, shining brightly.

"I'll make sure it doesn't dry out too much," chimes Truth.

Compassion and Truth work together to make sure things are just fine. Since things seem to be under control, Robot yawns and decides to get some sleep.

Robot awakens in horror, rubbing his eyes. Apparently, this world under Compassion and Truth is a messy place. It is a place of unchecked chaos.

"What have you done?" Robot asks the sun and the rain. "This disordered, unruly world is filled with overgrown things. Please leave and send me the wind!"

As the sun and rain leave, the wind enters.

"You've called for me in the nick of time. I'm also known as Justice. I'll cast aside these dangerously overgrown vines," says the wind.

And so Justice begins to blow.

"Leave everything to me. I'll protect you from these overgrown vines," says Justice.

"Thanks!" replies Robot.

Justice starts to blow harder, and the overgrown vines begin to scatter.

Justice blows even harder and, as ever-stronger winds are unleashed, the temperature drops.

The overgrow vines are swept away as ever-increasing, swirling, icy winds engulf Robot.

Justice blows yet harder. Robot is hurtled into the air. "Did you just blow so hard that you flipped the world upside-down?" asks Robot.

"Oops..." says Justice. "I guess the whole world just revolted."

Without Compassion or Truth, but with Justice fully unleashed, Robot discovers an upside-down world in full revolt.

"Oh, gosh, I seem to be making a mess of things. Please send me some sunshine. I certainly need it. I'm closing my eyes. When I open them, please let things be better," pleads Robot.

However, the results were not what Robot wanted. Despite having Compassion and Justice, the new world lacked Truth. Thus, it became a world of injustice.

In this new world of injustice, even gifts of goodies and sweets are surrounded by long needles! Unhappy with the sun, Robot impulsively decides to swap out the sun for rain, hoping for the best.

"Send me Truth now!" exclaims Robot.

However, in a world of only Truth and Justice but without any Compassion, Robot finds a world of rain and wind but no sunshine —a world of arrogance.

Robot asks, "Boot, can you see anything out of those shades? I simply see a world of arrogance."

"I've failed. Nothing works." sighs Robot.

"I fear I've failed you, too," says Justice, as the winds continue to swirl.

"Relax, old friends. Maybe it's not a question of actually asking, but simply being ready for 'it,' and then 'it' happens," says Truth.

"Yes, I should not have been so self-absorbed. I did not appreciate every one of you nearly enough. Now I miss the sun, and I wish I had not dismissed my old friend. At least we would have had each other," says Robot, mournfully.

The sun suddenly appears and says, "I got to thinking the other day and was wondering how my young friend was doing. I thought I'd stop by today. I hope you don't mind."

"Mind? I am so happy to see you, Compassion! Now that I have my three friends together, I feel so much better," declares Robot.

"We find you changed for the better. We are happy to spend time with you by our own choice. Sleep now, for you've struggled mightily in the last few days," chime the wind, sun, and rain.

Robot sleeps a long, deep, and sweet sleep. Robot awakens to a wondrous, beautiful scene, where lollipops fly thorough the air, and candy grows on trees.

"What happened?" asks Robot.

"My friends and I worked our magic while you slept," replies Truth.

"But I wish I had helped," says Robot.

"But you did. None of this would have been possible without the sweat of your previous efforts," Compassion responds.

"...and the power of your dreams," continues Justice.

"If you want something badly enough, sometimes it comes true," concludes Compassion.

For when Compassion, Truth and Justice come together, they can create the enchanted village of Balance.

"I now have everything I ever wanted, but I wish I had a proper name, too," sighs Robot.

"You shall be called Echo. For a good word does not die — it inspires. It begins to echo in the heart. When it finds fertile ground, it lays root, and then the cycle starts anew," declares Compassion (whose other name was Love).

And so Echo and the three friends formed a new, wonderful family and lived happily ever after.

Bonus Section

Where are they now?

Echo has been working on a stone tablet at the entrance of the village detailing this adventure.

	Wind	Rain	Sun	
	JUSTICE	TRUTH	COMPASSION /LOVE	RESULT
	No	No	No	Lost
	No	No	Yes	Ineffective
	No	Yes	No	Insensitive
	No	Yes	Yes	Chaos
	Yes	No	No	Revolt
	Yes	No	Yes	Injustice
	Yes	Yes	No	Arrogance
	Yes	Yes	Yes	Balance

How about Echo's friends?

Well they now have their own bookstore.
Echo likes to drop by now and then.

THE END

If you liked this book, check out other books by the author at www.fuadakamal.com.

www.ingramcontent.com/pod-product-compliance
Lightning Source LLC
Chambersburg PA
CBHW041545240626

47164CB00003B/138